Santa's Littlest Helper Travels the World

First published in Great Britain in 2007 by Bloomsbury Publishing Plc,
36 Soho Square, London, W1D 3QY

First published in Germany in 2006 by Carl Hanser Verlag GmbH & Co KG
Vilshofener Strasse 10, D-81679, Munich, Germany

Original title:
Der kleine Weihnachtsmann reist um die Welt

Copyright © Carl Hanser Verlag München Wien 2006

A CIP catalogue record of this book is available from the British Library

ISBN 978 0 7475 9359 1

Printed in China by South China Printing Co.

1 3 5 7 9 10 8 6 4 2

All papers used by Bloomsbury Publishing are natural, recyclable products
made from wood grown in well-managed forests. The manufacturing processes
conform to the environmental regulations of the country of origin.

Santa's Littlest Helper Travels the World

Anu Stohner * Henrike Wilson

BLOOMSBURY
CHILDREN'S
BOOKS

In a little village far far to the north, Santa and his Helpers were very very busy – just like every year. They were wrapping presents, baking mince pies, polishing the sleighs and grooming the reindeer. It was a hive of activity!

But one of Santa's Helpers had started preparing long before the others. He had finished packing his sleigh and even had enough time to build a lovely big snowman. He was, of course, Santa's Littlest Helper!

The other Helpers moaned
because they still had so much
to do.
"We've only three more
days to go! Can't you give
us a hand?" they asked the
Littlest Helper.
"Why should I?" he teased.
"It's all right for some!"
said the other Helpers.

The Littlest Helper chuckled and then happily joined in loading the sleighs anyway. Every year they helped Santa deliver presents to children around the world – everyone except for Santa's Littlest Helper. He had the special job of delivering presents to all the animals.

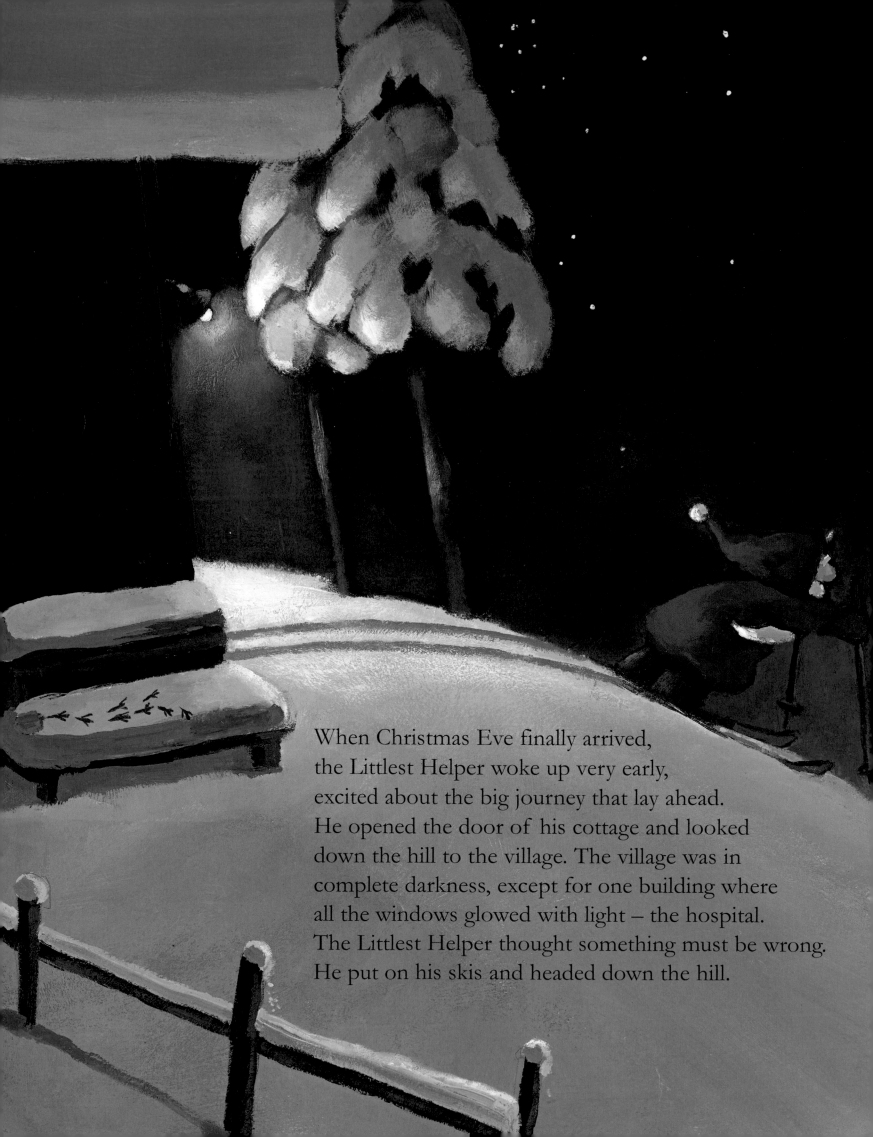

When Christmas Eve finally arrived,
the Littlest Helper woke up very early,
excited about the big journey that lay ahead.
He opened the door of his cottage and looked
down the hill to the village. The village was in
complete darkness, except for one building where
all the windows glowed with light – the hospital.
The Littlest Helper thought something must be wrong.
He put on his skis and headed down the hill.

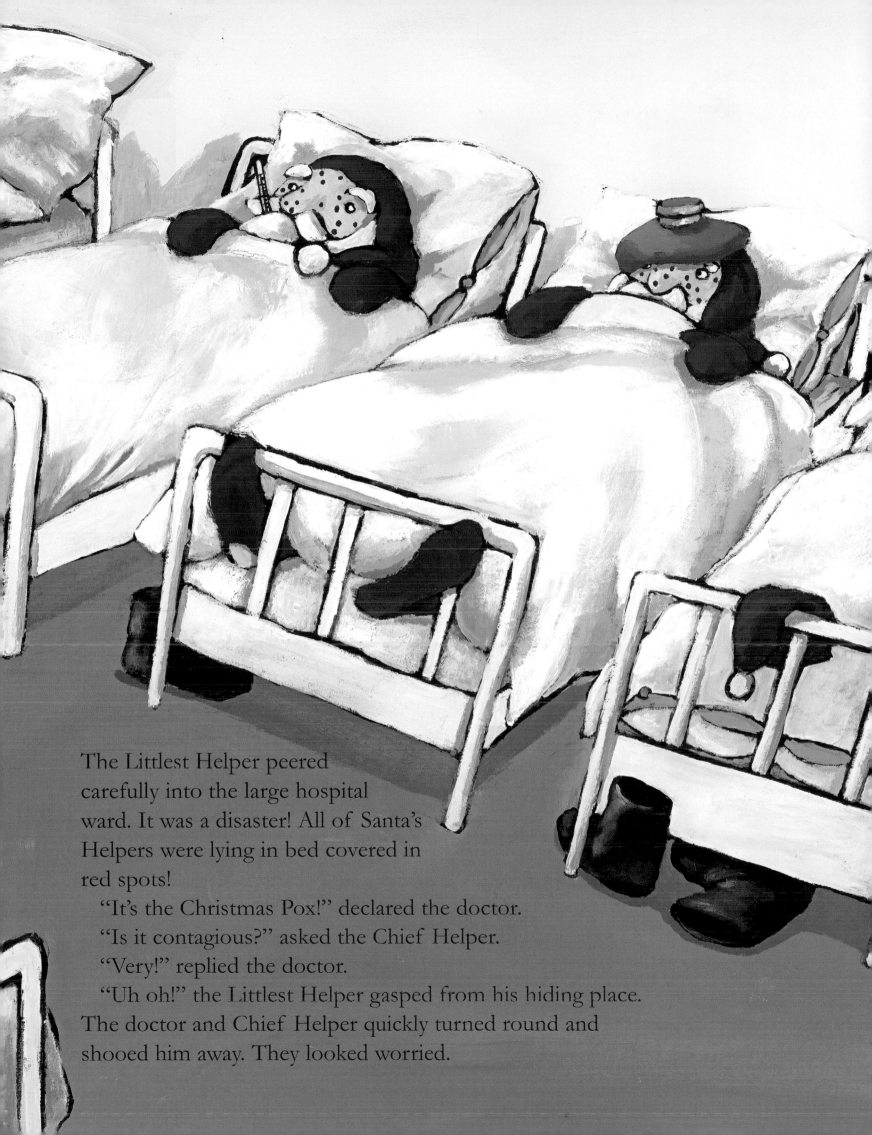

The Littlest Helper peered
carefully into the large hospital
ward. It was a disaster! All of Santa's
Helpers were lying in bed covered in
red spots!

"It's the Christmas Pox!" declared the doctor.
"Is it contagious?" asked the Chief Helper.
"Very!" replied the doctor.
"Uh oh!" the Littlest Helper gasped from his hiding place.
The doctor and Chief Helper quickly turned round and
shooed him away. They looked worried.

It would be impossible for the Chief Helper and the
Littlest Helper to visit all the children alone. And the
doctor must stay at home and look after his patients.
But the Littlest Helper had an idea.

"I've got it! Let's ask the animals to help!" he said
to the Chief Helper.

"The animals?" said the Chief Helper. "Of course,
what a wonderful idea! But you will have to ask
them," he said, "they'll only listen to you."

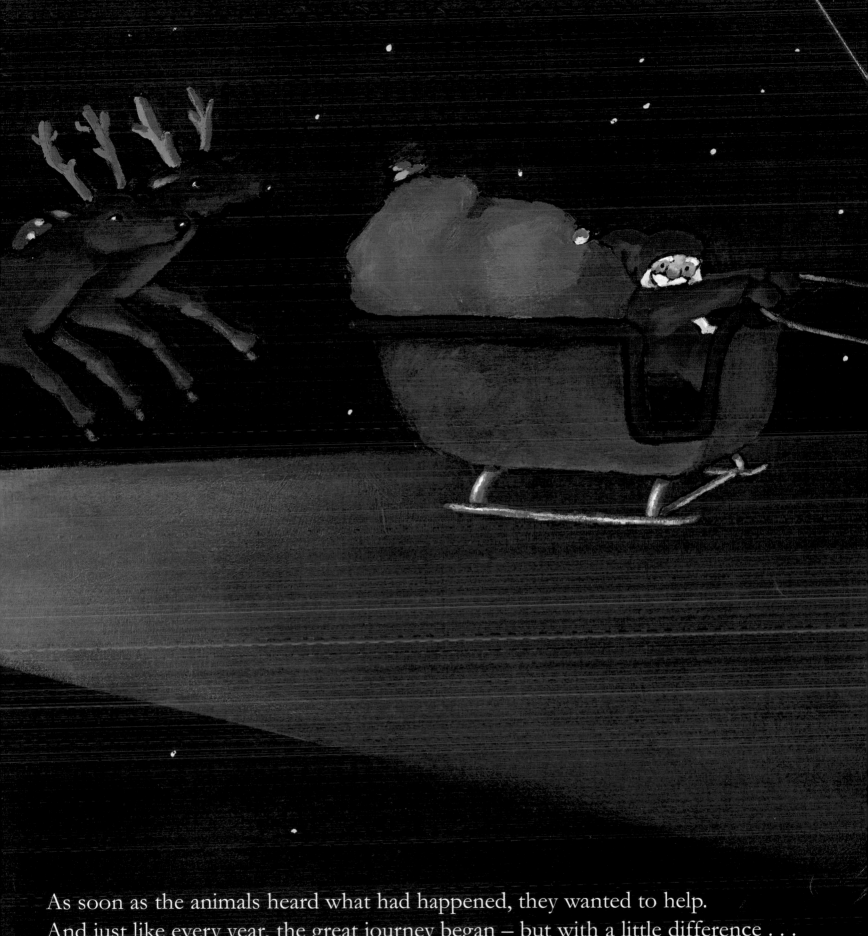

As soon as the animals heard what had happened, they wanted to help.
And just like every year, the great journey began – but with a little difference . . .
As Santa, Chief Helper, bear, fox and all the other animals took the reins of
their sleighs, they set off across the great blanket of ice in the north – past
mountains, valleys and rivers towards the biggest cities and the smallest villages.
And the Littlest Helper was in the lead!

In one city the buildings were so tall that the owl felt light-headed, but she didn't let it show. Only the city mouse she was carrying on her back thought he noticed a teeny-weeny tremble.

In the next city stood a huge tower made completely of iron. Elk wanted to know what it was for.

"For absolutely nothing – it's just beautiful," said the clever fox.

"Just like the antlers on his head," giggled the field mouse, but luckily the elk couldn't hear him.

Another city was built in the sea, and the streets were made of big and small canals instead of roads.

"Hopefully no one will fall in the water!" said the Chief Helper.

"Have no fear," grumbled the bear, "we can swim."

The rabbit said nothing, and only the Littlest Helper saw how nervously he scratched one of his long ears with his back paw.

Only once did the Littlest Helper
get carried away with the excitement.
He went under a bridge rather than
flying over the top, as it ought to be
done. But the Chief Helper didn't
mind too much – not tonight!

Through the long night they flew without rest.
When dawn slowly crept over the horizon, the Chief
Helper climbed stiffly from his sleigh. He thought quietly
to himself that he was a little old for such adventures. Next
year he would send the other Helpers for immunization shots,
and then maybe he could stay at home and drink mulled wine.

Back home at last, the Chief Helper
settled into his armchair with a mug
of mulled wine. He thanked the
Littlest Helper for his brilliant idea
and for all his hard work.

Santa's Littlest Helper drank hot blueberry juice
and there were as many Christmas treats as he
could possibly hope to eat! Now, finally, it was
time for the animals to receive their presents.
Everyone had a wonderful time, and only
the badger missed out – he was so tired
he fell asleep before the presents
were unwrapped.

Unfortunately, back in the hospital, the sick Helpers only got a little soup and medicine.

"At least another week in bed," said the doctor sternly.

"Can't we have gingerbread?" they asked. "It's supposed to be good for you."

"Not for Christmas Pox," said the doctor – and he would know.
   They grumbled a bit, but comforted themselves with the thought of New Year's punch!

And the children? They were overjoyed with their presents
and didn't even notice the unusual Helpers on Christmas Eve.
Only one little boy, called Jack, had woken up and secretly
peeped out of his window. Since then he has tried to tell
his friends that Santa Claus looks a little bit like an elk.
But of course no one believes him!